14

BIBLIOGRAPHY
Pirate Treasures

For Quinton (of course)
—A.E.C.

For Edith Lieberman
—E.S.

VIKING
Published by Penguin Group
Penguin Young Readers Group, 345 Hudson Street,
New York, New York 10014, U.S.A.
Penguin Books Ltd, 80 Strand, London WC2R 0RL, England
Penguin Books Australia Ltd, 250 Camberwell Road,
Camberwell, Victoria 3124, Australia
Penguin Books Canada Ltd, 10 Alcorn Avenue, Toronto, Ontario, Canada M4V 3B2
Penguin Books (N.Z.) Ltd, 182-190 Wairau Road, Auckland 10, New Zealand

First published in 2004 by Viking, a division of Penguin Young Readers Group

1 3 5 7 9 10 8 6 4 2

LIBRARY OF CONGRESS CATALOGING-IN-PUBLICATION DATA
Cannon, A. E. (Ann Edwards)
Let the good times roll with Pirate Pete and Pirate Joe /
by A.E. Cannon ; illustrated by Elwood H. Smith.
p. cm.
Summary: Pirate Pete and Pirate Joe visit the Pirate Queen and have fun
playing games and going to Disco Dan's House of Pins until it is bedtime
and the Pirate Queen becomes just their mother once again.
ISBN 0-670-03679-X (Hardcover)
[1. Mothers and sons—Fiction. 2. Pirates—Fiction. 3. Humorous stories.]
I. Smith, Elwood H., date-, ill. II. Title.
PZ7.C17135Le 2004   [E]—dc22   2003010820

Viking® and Easy-to-Read® are registered trademarks of Penguin Group (USA) Inc.

Manufactured in China
Set in Bookman, Slappy

Reading level 2.1

Pirate Pete and Pirate Joe Search for the Pirate Queen

This is Pirate Pete.

This is Pirate Joe.

Every day Pirate Pete and Pirate Joe

do their pirate chores.

JoB List FoR
PIRATE PETE + PIRATE JOE
① Dig up buried treasure.
② open treasure chest and take out coins.
③ Count coins forwards.
④ Count coins backwards.
⑤ Put coins back in treasure chest.
⑥ Bury buried treasure.

"We work hard!" says Pirate Pete.

When their chores are done,

the pirates like to play.

"We play hard!" says Pirate Joe.

Today the pirates want to play

at the Pirate Queen's lighthouse.

Pirate Pete calls for the pirate pets.

"Yo, pirate dog Dudley!

Yo, pirate cat Studley!

Yo, pirate parrot Bucko!"

"Time to rock! Time to roll!"

says Pirate Joe.

The pirates and their pets get into a van.

It is big.

It is black.

It has cool wheels.

It is called the Jolly Roger.

Yo ho ho and away they go!

"The Pirate Queen is NOT sweet,"

says Pirate Pete.

"The Pirate Queen has stinky feet,"

says Pirate Joe.

"Yo ho!" say Pirate Pete and Pirate Joe.

"That is good enough for us!"

The pirates drive to the

Pirate Queen's lighthouse.

It is tall. It has stairs that go up

and stairs that go down.

It sits on a small island near the shore.

The shore is covered with signs.

The pirates park the Jolly Roger.

They go inside the lighthouse.

"Ding-dong!" they say. "Pirates calling!"

No one answers.

"Where is the Pirate Queen?" asks Pirate Pete.

Dudley barks.

Pirate Pete moans and Pirate Joe groans.

They are afraid, and their knees knock.

Knock! Knock!

"Who's there?" asks Pirate Joe.

"We are there!" says Pirate Pete.

"Let's find the Pirate Queen!"

"Yo ho!" says Pirate Joe.

The pirates rattle their swords.

"Aargh!" say Pirate Pete and Pirate Joe.

The pirates look upstairs.

The pirates look downstairs.

"No Pirate Queen!" says Pirate Pete.

"Aargh!" says Pirate Joe.

The pirates look on top of her bed.

They look under her bed.

"No Pirate Queen!" says Pirate Pete.

"Bigger aargh!" says Pirate Joe.

The pirates go outside.

They look in her hot tub.

They look in her fishing pond.

"No Pirate Queen!" says Pirate Pete.

"Biggest aargh!" says Pirate Joe.

The pirates go inside.

Just then the Pirate Queen walks in
with her pet stunt duck, Duck-O.
Her arms are filled with bags and boxes.
They are filled with eels and crabs!
Yo ho! The Pirate Queen has been
shopping!

When she sees Pirate Pete and

Pirate Joe, she dances a jig.

"AHOY, BOYS!" booms the Pirate Queen.

"We thought you were gone,"

says Pirate Pete.

"We thought you ran away,"

says Pirate Joe.

"AARGH!" booms the Pirate Queen.

"I AM NOT GOING! I AM NOT
RUNNING! YOU ARE MY PIRATES!
I AM YOUR MOTHER!"

"Yo ho ho!" say Pirate Pete and Pirate
Joe. "LET THE GOOD TIMES ROLL!"

The Pirate Queen hugs Pirate Pete
and Pirate Joe.

The Pirate Queen hugs Duck-O.

"Quack! Quack!" says Duck-O.

Duck-O stands on his head.

"It's Good to Be Queen!"

"WHO'S HUNGRY?" booms the

Pirate Queen.

"I am hungry for crabs," says Pirate Pete.

"I am hungry for eels," says Pirate Joe.

"FOLLOW ME, BOYS!

I'LL COOK YOU SOME GRUB!"

Pirate Pete and Pirate Joe follow

the Pirate Queen into the kitchen.

"BELLY UP TO THE TABLE!" booms

the Pirate Queen.

The pirates sit down.

Pirate Pete eats crabs.

Pirate Joe eats eels.

The Pirate Queen eats jellyfish on toast.

"M-M-M-M-M-M-M!" say these pirates.

"WHAT SHOULD WE DO NOW?"

booms the Pirate Queen.

"Let's play pirate games!" says

Pirate Joe.

Pirate Pete, Pirate Joe, the Pirate Queen,

and the pirate pets play

"Ring around the Pirate."

Duck-O does a back flip.

"THAT WAS FUN!" booms the Pirate

Queen. "WHAT SHOULD WE DO NOW?"

They all play "Pin the Tail on Pirate Joe."

"THAT WAS FUN!" booms the Pirate

Queen. "WHAT SHOULD WE DO NOW?"

The pirates find words that rhyme

with "grog."

"Jog," says Pirate Pete.

"FROG!" booms the Pirate Queen.

"Big fat smelly pirate hog!" says

Pirate Joe.

"I KNOW WHAT WE SHOULD DO

NOW!" booms the Pirate Queen.

"FOLLOW ME, BOYS!"

"Yo ho!" say Pirate Pete and Pirate Joe.

The pirates and their pets get in the
Jolly Roger. They drive forward.

"PIRATES!" booms the Pirate Queen.

"HERE TODAY! GONE TOMORROW!"

"Aargh!" say Pirate Pete and Pirate Joe.

They drive backwards. The Pirate

Queen gets into the Jolly Roger.

"Yo ho!" say the pirates.

And away they all go!

"These Pirates Rock! These Pirates Bowl!"

The pirates drive to Disco Dan's

House of Pins.

Drive, pirates, drive!

Inside, music is playing.

Bright lights are flashing.

People are bowling.

People are dancing.

Pirate Joe is afraid.

He knows how to limbo.

He does not know how to bowl.

"AHOY, DISCO DAN!" booms the
Pirate Queen. "MEET MY BOYS!"

"We are mean!" says Pirate Pete.

"We are not clean!" says Pirate Joe.

"We are not sweet!" says Pirate Pete.

"We have stinky feet!" says Pirate Joe.

"AHOY, BOYS!" booms the Pirate
Queen. "MEET MY MAN, DAN!"

"You spin the ball," says Disco Dan.

"I spin the tunes."

Music is playing.

Bright lights are flashing.

The pirates start clapping.

The pirates start dancing.

Pirate Pete does the hornpipe.

Pirate Joe does the limbo.

Disco Dan does the moonwalk.

The moonwalk

"WE NEED A LANE, DISCO DAN!"

booms the Pirate Queen.

"Put on these shirts.

Put on these shoes.

Moonwalk this way!" says Disco Dan.

Pirate Pete does the moonwalk.

The Pirate Queen does the moonwalk.

Pirate Joe is afraid.

He knows how to moonwalk.

He does not know how to bowl.

"COME ON BABY!" booms the Pirate

Queen. "LUCK BE A LADY!"

The Pirate Queen rolls the ball.

Crash go all the pins.

"STRIKE!" says Disco Dan.

Pirate Pete rolls the ball.

Crash go all the pins.

"STRIKE!" says Disco Dan.

It's Pirate Joe's turn.

He looks at the ball.

"What if I miss the pins?" says Pirate Joe. "What if I look silly?"

"We all miss sometimes," says Disco Dan. "Do not be afraid."

Pirate Joe rolls the ball.

It does not roll fast.

It does not roll straight.

It hits one pin.

"AHOY, MY BOY!

THAT'S GOOD ENOUGH FOR ME!"

booms the Pirate Queen.

"Yo ho ho and a bottle of pop!"

says Pirate Pete.

Pirate Joe rolls the ball again and

again. *Crash* go all the pins.

"I love this game!" says Pirate Joe.

Duck-O does a cartwheel

AND the splits.

The pirates dance. The pirates bowl.

The pirates rock. The pirates roll.

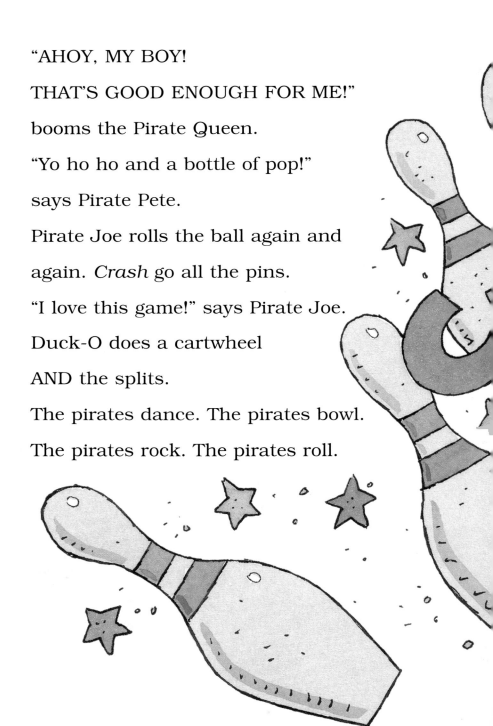

Outside, the moon climbs high.

It shines bright upon the sea.

"AHOY, BOYS!" booms the Pirate

Queen. "TIME TO GO!"

"No, no," say Pirate Pete and Pirate Joe.

"Now, now," says Disco Dan. "Mind

your mother."

"See you later, alligator,"

says Pirate Pete.

"In a while, crocodile," says Pirate Joe.

"Pretty soon, baboon," says Disco Dan.

The pirate crew get in the Jolly Roger.

"LET'S HAVE A SLEEPOVER!"

booms the Pirate Queen.

"TO THE LIGHTHOUSE!"

The pirates drive to the lighthouse

and go inside.

They take off their patches and

put on their pajamas.

They sip warm milk.

They read a bedtime story.

They go to sleep.

The Pirate Queen turns out the

lighthouse light.

"Good night, boys," she does not boom.

JUV
READER
Cannon   **Cannon, A. E.**

Let the good
times roll with
Pirate Pete and

DUE DATE
